LEADERS LIKE US

BAYARD *Rustin*

BY J. P. MILLER

ILLUSTRATED BY
MARKIA JENAI

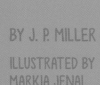

Rourke
Educational Media

A Division of
Carson
Dellosa
Education

Before Reading: *Building Background Knowledge and Vocabulary*

Building background knowledge can help children process new information and build upon what they already know. Before reading a book, it is important to tap into what children already know about the topic. This will help them develop their vocabulary and increase their reading comprehension.

Questions and Activities to Build Background Knowledge:

1. Look at the front cover of the book and read the title. What do you think this book will be about?
2. What do you already know about this topic?
3. Take a book walk and skim the pages. Look at the table of contents, photographs, captions, and bold words. Did these text features give you any information or predictions about what you will read in this book?

Vocabulary: *Vocabulary Is Key to Reading Comprehension*

Use the following directions to prompt a conversation about each word.

- Read the vocabulary words.
- What comes to mind when you see each word?
- What do you think each word means?

> ## Vocabulary Words:
> - *activists*
> - *boycotts*
> - *Civil Rights Movement*
> - *discrimination*
> - *equality*
> - *protest*
> - *Quaker*
> - *slavery*

During Reading: *Reading for Meaning and Understanding*

To achieve deep comprehension of a book, children are encouraged to use close reading strategies. During reading, it is important to have children stop and make connections. These connections result in deeper analysis and understanding of a book.

 Close Reading a Text

During reading, have children stop and talk about the following:

- Any confusing parts
- Any unknown words
- Text to text, text to self, text to world connections
- The main idea in each chapter or heading

Encourage children to use context clues to determine the meaning of any unknown words. These strategies will help children learn to analyze the text more thoroughly as they read.

When you are finished reading this book, turn to the next-to-last page for **Text-Dependent Questions** and an **Extension Activity**.

TABLE OF CONTENTS

THE MARCH ON WASHINGTON......................4

BECOMING AN ACTIVIST 8

LEADING FROM BEHIND
THE SCENES 14

TIME LINE 21

GLOSSARY 22

INDEX 23

TEXT-DEPENDENT QUESTIONS.................23

EXTENSION ACTIVITY........................23

ABOUT THE AUTHOR
AND ILLUSTRATOR...........................24

THE MARCH ON WASHINGTON

Think of a time when something seemed unfair.
How did you feel? What did you do? Bayard Rustin
knew about working to fix unfair things.

On August 28, 1963, daylight stretched across
the city. Engines roared and horns honked. The
people of Washington, DC, were starting a new day.

But Bayard Rustin was already hard at work. He had spent months planning the March on Washington for Jobs and Freedom. The big day was finally here.

The clock ticked. Bayard was worried. What if people did not come?

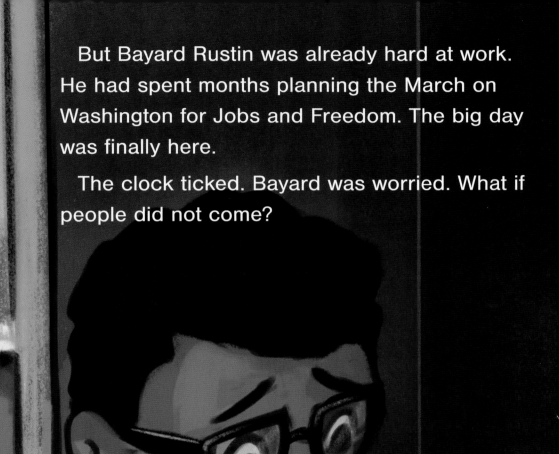

He did not worry for long. Hundreds of thousands of people were ready to **protest**. Black and white people walked arm-in-arm. They were tired of **discrimination** in America.

That day at the event, Dr. Martin Luther King Jr. gave his famous "I Have a Dream" speech. His speech gave many African Americans hope.

BECOMING AN ACTIVIST

Bayard Rustin was born in 1912. **Slavery** had been against the law for 47 years. But black people were still not treated as equal to white people. Bayard's grandparents, Janifer and Julia Rustin, were **activists** for equal rights. He learned from them.

Hotels near Bayard's family did not let African American people stay there. Janifer and Julia Rustin let visiting leaders stay with them instead. The visitors were part of the **Civil Rights Movement**. Bayard met these leaders and learned from them too.

Famous Guests

The Rustin family had some famous guests when Bayard was young. The activists W.E.B. Du Bois and James Weldon Johnson came to visit many times.

At that time, black and white children had to go to different schools. Signs on buses told black people where to sit. They had to drink from different water fountains. It was the law. But it wasn't fair.

Bayard wanted to work for **equality**. He had learned from his grandmother's **Quaker** beliefs. He went to college with the help of the African Methodist Episcopal church. He was going to be a leader.

LEADING FROM BEHIND THE SCENES

Bayard believed in solving problems without violence. He made friends who felt the same way he did. He began teaching other people. He helped them plan peaceful protests, **boycotts**, and other events.

Between the 1940s and 1970s, black people **marched,**

...boycotted,

...went to jail,

...and died for equal rights.

A Peaceful Life

Bayard learned about being nonviolent from Mahatma Gandhi. He was a lawyer and activist in India. He believed in fixing problems with peace.

Bayard Rustin had a special place in the Civil Rights Movement. He did not give famous speeches like some people. Instead, he planned and organized. He helped people run equal rights groups. He showed them how to fight unfair laws without being violent.

Some people treated Bayard unfairly because he was gay, but this did not stop him. The police arrested Bayard several times for his protests, but he did not quit.

Bayard helped organize the March on Washington for Jobs and Freedom. It was the biggest march he had ever worked on. Bayard was an important leader on that important day. He helped make big changes for the Civil Rights Movement and for the United States.

Bayard's work didn't end once the March on Washington was over. He continued to work hard, organize, and lead, all from behind the scenes.

Bayard believed that nonviolent work for equality could change the world. He proved that there are many ways to be an important leader and make a difference.

"We need in every community a group of angelic troublemakers."
—Bayard Rustin

TIME LINE

1912   Bayard Rustin is born on March 17th.

1932   Bayard starts school at Wilberforce University in Wilberforce, Ohio.

1936   Bayard is asked to leave Wilberforce after protesting school conditions.

1937   Bayard starts school at City College of New York in New York City.

1942   Bayard begins traveling the country talking about civil rights.

1944   Bayard is arrested for missing a meeting that could send him to war.

1945   Bayard organizes the Free India Committee for India's independence from Great Britain.

1947   Bayard tests laws against discrimination. He is arrested.

1955   Bayard meets Dr. Martin Luther King Jr. and talks with him about nonviolence.

1956   Bayard helps Dr. Martin Luther King Jr. with the Montgomery Bus Boycott.

1963   Bayard helps organize the March on Washington for Jobs and Freedom. Over 200,000 people attend.

1964   Bayard becomes an advisor to the Mississippi Freedom Democratic Party.

1964   Bayard helps create the A. Philip Randolph Institute, named for his mentor, the noted labor and civil rights activist.

1987   Bayard dies on August 24th at age 75.

2013   Bayard is awarded the Presidential Medal of Freedom after his death by President Barack Obama.

GLOSSARY

activists (AK-tiv-ists): people who work for political or social change

boycotts (BOI-kahts): refusals to do business with a company as a punishment or protest

Civil Rights Movement (SIV-uhl rites MOOV-muhnt): a political movement for equality that was very important in the 1960s

discrimination (dis-krim-i-NAY-shuhn): unfair treatment of others based on differences in such things as age, race, or gender

equality (i-KWAH-li-tee): the right of everyone to be treated the same, with no one getting special advantages

protest (PROH-test): to make a demonstration or statement against something

Quaker (KWAY-kur): a name for the Religious Society of Friends, a group based on peace

slavery (SLAY-vur-ee): a system in which some people claim to own others and force them to work

INDEX

arrested 17

buses 12

college 12

Dr. Martin Luther King Jr. 7

equal rights 8

Mahatma Gandhi 15

March on Washington for Jobs and Freedom 5, 18, 20

organize(d) 16, 18, 20

TEXT-DEPENDENT QUESTIONS

1. What event did Bayard Rustin plan for August 28th, 1963?
2. What are some ways that Bayard Rustin worked for equal rights?
3. What was the March on Washington for Jobs and Freedom about?
4. Where did Bayard Rustin learn about being nonviolent?
5. Why did guests stay with Bayard Rustin's grandparents?

EXTENSION ACTIVITY

Choose an issue you feel strongly about. Maybe it is bullying at your school or litter in your neighborhood. Think about how you could lead an event to help make people aware of the issue. Write down every step you would need to take to plan and organize the event.

ABOUT THE AUTHOR

J. P. Miller is a debut author in children's picture books. She is eager to write stories about little- and well-known African American leaders. She hopes that her stories will augment the classroom experience, educate, and inspire readers. J. P. lives in Metro Atlanta, Georgia, and enjoys playing pickleball and swimming in her spare time.

ABOUT THE ILLUSTRATOR

Markia Jenai was raised in Detroit during rough times, but she found adventure through art and storytelling. She grew up listening to old stories of her family members, which gave her an interest in history. Drawing was her way of exploring the world through imagination.

www.rourkeeducationalmedia.com

Quote source: *Brother Outsider: The Life of Bayard Rustin.* The American Documentary, 2003.

Edited by: Tracie Santos
Illustrations by: Markia Jenai
Cover and interior layout by: Rhea Magaro-Wallace

Library of Congress PCN Data

Bayard Rustin / J. P. Miller
(Leaders Like Us)
ISBN 978-1-73163-801-4 (hard cover)
ISBN 978-1-73163-878-6 (soft cover)
ISBN 978-1-73163-955-4 (e-Book)
ISBN 978-1-73164-032-1 (ePub)
Library of Congress Control Number: 2020930060

Rourke Educational Media
Printed in the United States of America
03-3052111937